Living in Dreamtime

~Usha~

Illustrations by Salil Sojwal

PERKY PARROT

NIYOGI BOOKS

First published by **PERKY PARROT**

An imprint of

NIYOGI BOOKS

Block D, Building No. 77

Okhla Industrial Area, Phase-I

New Delhi-110 020, INDIA

Tel: 91-11-26816301, 26818960

Email: niyogibooks@gmail.com

Website: www.niyogibooksindia.com

Editor: Sucharita Ghosh

Design: Shashi Bhushan Prasad

Cover and illustrations: Salil Sojwal

ISBN: 978-93-91125-83-7

Publication: 2022

Printed at Niyogi Offset Pvt. Ltd., New Delhi, India

"To my uncle who brought me up"

A FISH OUT OF WATER

Parina watched anxiously as they lowered the long black box into the freshly dug hole. Her Master was in the box. He was sleeping since yesterday. Not a sound from him. Not even a snore. He hadn't stirred once. Even her fish had been brought to her by a complete stranger.

Strange, she thought now. Weird, worrying… Master had never been this careless before. Forgetting to bring her food and sleeping so late. Dang!

Since morning, she'd been waiting for him to wake up and fetch her food. But the cock had crowed; the wooden cuckoo had sung its full song; the sun had finished half his journey across the sky sending shadows into hiding everywhere; sunlight had broken through the semi-circular glass wall, climbed down the glass roof, jumped in through the two windows and wiped out all trace of yesternight. But Master had slept on.

Having missed her morning meal, she was ravenous. She had no intention of waiting for her meal till evening. After a long four-hour wait, at exactly half-past noon, just after the cuckoo's call, she'd kicked up the racket that had brought her Master's son running into the room.

But now, the shadows had grown thin and long. The sun had ripened and was hanging precariously low in the sky. Very soon, he would hang from the trees—orange in hue. Even her Master had changed position. He had moved into a custom-made box with sheaths of roses wrapped around him.

Uneasiness darted a squeamish finger up her back. She tried recalling the previous day's events. Master had woken up as usual when the cock had given his routine battle-cry, the earth-shattering noise jolting the early birds into action.

Jumpstart Rooster had cock-a-doodled for a whole minute, and then repeated it for the ones who hadn't been moved by his performance the first time around. She'd named him Jumpstart after a noisy breakfast show that always made her jump out of her skin.

These birds take their proverbs too literally, she muttered under her breath. As far as she knew, one would always run into worms, at all times, in all places. You don't want to go hunting for them at an unearthly hour. But the next second, her meandering thoughts returned to her Master like a fish towards water. He had woken to Jumpstart's alarm and freshened up.

He'd then come over and talked to her. She remembered him cribbing. He'd teased her about her weight, reminding her about the sweet little thing she'd once been, complaining that she was now fat and heavy. That is why he's stopped taking her out, he declared. She remembered him saying something nasty too—that maybe he pampered her, feeding her whenever she threw a tantrum. If she had to hunt for her own fish, she would have been a lot slimmer, he'd grumbled.

He'd then cracked a couple of jokes about her weight and burst into laughter. She hadn't listened, wondering about what he'd said. She hated being called fat and she'd just remembered that she still hadn't had her morning meal. She wanted to sulk but watching Master laugh made her laugh too. She started laughing. Watching her laugh at a joke at her expense, Master launched into a fresh bout of laughter. Contagious laughter was a game they played too often—an exercise to lighten the heart. They laughed till they rolled over and nearly split their sides. Tears welled in their eyes and were about to spill when suddenly hunger pangs knocked and silenced Parina's laughter.

Happy tears took on a guise and threatened to dissolve into something dangerous. Crumpling her face but still managing to keep her pout, she observed that the frequency of her feed was competing with the number of hair on his shiny, bald head. She had meant to be offensive, of course, but Master had burst out laughing again, said, 'Touché', and had gone out of the room, returning in a few minutes with a bucketful of fish.

Unceremoniously, he'd thrown them in her barrel, unperturbed about the half-flooded room or the water slowly trickling out of the slit in her glass globe.

He had then sat at his desk, opened what he called the world's largest bestseller, and began reading aloud, pausing once in a way to preach. He had barely finished a verse when hunger pangs rang the bell in reminder. Parina answered the call of her wild belly, chased a salmon and wolfed it down.

Hearing the commotion she created, he stopped and rebuked her for paying scant attention to the holy words and for eating without thanking the Lord. What he didn't know was that she could have recited it out to him, she had heard it that many times. And she didn't particularly like the book, dismissing it as a little too self-centred. Man calling himself the best of God's creation. Bah!

Also, the very idea of a man being able to part the sea by just raising a stick made her gurgle with laughter. It was a good story, but it made her think. She normally paid attention when he came to the part where the hero divides a few small fish amongst thousands of men. She couldn't help wondering how big 'small' was in those days. And then she would withdraw into her own lost world, longing for the freedom of a big ocean and chasing fish to comfort herself.

Parina shifted now, a little uncomfortable, wondering if she should've paid more attention to her

Master. She felt guilty, she must have really irritated him. But then during the last five years they had had their share of fights and Master had gone to bed angry, but he'd always woken up on time, brought her fish, taken her out...

But anyway, how could he get so angry just because she hadn't listened to him preach. Wasn't religion meant for mankind, so they can follow some rules, a code of conduct? Was it relevant to her species, to her? She wondered and hoped not. She was too curious about the world outside to sit at home and brood.

Moreover, she also had to practice catching fish. What if Master got so angry he actually carried out his threats? He wouldn't get her any fish and throw her back into the ocean? He'd threatened her yesterday, too, she remembered. Angry at her indifference, Master had remarked that if she didn't like being here and chose to live in her own world, he would put her back into the ocean the very same day.

Then in a huff, he'd gone to catch his afternoon nap, while she continued playing chase with the remaining fish.

At six in the evening, they'd stepped out with the intention of a long walk. That's what it would have been and should have been. But Master was still angry and sulking; she dared not ask him for a long walk, just getting out would be fine.

They'd gone towards the park with the jumping fish fountain. But at the turning, he'd spotted an old friend and stopped for a chat while she'd scared the wits off the friend's dog. She was a thoroughly decent, domesticated creature. She hadn't jumped and splashed the water, but had coughed up a misty fountain and clicked loudly instead.

She grinned now, remembering the look on the dog's face. The dog's jaw had almost hit the ground. Gosh! What kind of a monster is this? A fountain that moves and makes authoritative human sounds?

He'd been growling ever since he'd smelt something fishy about her. Parina was sure he hadn't expected her to be bigger than him because he'd tucked his tail between his legs the moment he'd seen her and pulled his master back home as quickly as possible.

After his friend's hurried departure, Master had wheeled her back into the house. He'd been quiet the whole evening, she'd noticed. Normally he talked a lot, telling her all the things she loved to hear. From Beethoven to the Bible. From the Koran to Kahlil Gibran. From the Vedas to the secrets of Shambala. Instead yesterday, he had turned on the television as soon as they'd stepped into the house.

They had watched silently as the heroine shed pretentious tears into a gentleman's stiff starched shirt. Soaking it wet and ruining it while the man ruffled her hair and assured her that it was all right, he loved her and would come back as soon as he earned enough money to look after her.

Calling it 'a stupid, sickening soap' Master had switched on the seven o' clock news he watched regularly. There was a new lady reading the news, looking delectable in her seaweed-grey dress—an admirable change from the shark-faced regulars with their toothy fake smiles.

However, immediately after the news Parina recalled that he'd gone out to return at nine. He had checked if she had enough fish for the night and without wishing her goodnight, turned the light off. He was still angry, she'd sensed.

At the flip of a switch, night entered and dropped a wet blanket on the room. Parina waited for her eyes to adjust to the darkness but fell asleep midway. Sometime early morning, she had woken up with a start, but after fixing her eyes on a blinking blue star, she'd drifted back to sleep, gently lolling in her waterbed.

The sun rose, the cock crowed, the cuckoo practised. But Master had slept on. He had never done that before. She was starving. But she'd waited for his regular lunch hour before she complained.

At half past noon, her stomach made threatening noises and she'd thumped heavily, splashing water everywhere in an effort to get him out of his deep slumber. But Master hadn't stirred.

The son had come running instead, hearing the storm she'd kicked up. He had yelled at her and turned to his father to complain about the racket. Instead, he'd stopped and reached out to shake him awake. 'Father!' he'd gasped and immediately jerked back as if Master had scalded him.

He'd flown into a rage, shaken his father violently, and run out of the room. He had looked very agitated, she remembered now.

Very soon, he'd returned with another man. The newcomer was a stranger in a white coat—with earplugs and wires connecting at his heart on a pendant. Some neighbours had also followed them inside. Some with curious eyes and sad faces. Some with sad eyes and long faces. They had looked worse, grave, when the man after touching the Master with his pendant had turned back and slowly shaken his head.

Just like in the movies, thought the dolphin now, when someone dies. The doctor comes in, checks and slowly shakes his head to say: Sorry, he is already dead. I'm helpless.

Everything fell into place as she plugged the gaps in her mind.

Master not waking up in spite of the storm she'd kicked up. The doctor stepping in. Shaking his head. Master being carried out. Some stranger getting fish for her, wheeling her here. The Master now resting in his bed of roses, the crowd gathering and now the hole in the ground. The burial.

Lord, this is a funeral! I'm at my Master's funeral without even being informed of his death! She wobbled trying to steer her mind.

Dead? Was Master really dead?

Horrified at her chain of thoughts, Parina stopped remembering. Is he dead? Was her Master dead? Gut-splitting pain seared through her like lightning. Her mind cleared. The fog that had blinded her for so long lifted. She was beginning to see the truth.

No! It isn't possible. How can such a thing happen! Master dying! Leaving me alone! Impossible!

He'd laughed like a mad man yesterday. He looked old but he was young, brimming with life. Suddenly how can he turn lifeless! A cold, inanimate object, never to laugh, never to talk, never to walk again.

A salty teardrop fell into the barrel. Rain, she thought vaguely. But deep inside her, acceptance took a seat. The son's distress, the doctor's presence, the crowd, the sorrowful crowd and the long black box being buried. Oh, what will I do, what will happen to me, she cried silently, wailing on a pitch out of human earshot.

She moaned an animal cry. Her blowhole gushed like a happy spring. She flayed her flippers. The whole gathering turned and stared at the dolphin with the permanent grin. Again, she splashed the water, this time deliberately. They turned back to the box. They don't know me, they don't realise that even I can feel pain.

Dizzy, her tired mind collapsed. The heart took over, released a spate of emotions, injecting tears in her eyes. Stunned and drained, she wailed alone in her glass globe.

Further ahead, near the priest, her Master's son stood with a pained expression on his thin long face. Even he was standing alone, a palm in a desert. Tall, thin and frail, not wanting to be there but determined to stand and do his duty.

She knew even he was crying inside. They were all remembering her Master. All the things he'd done. Dusting the unpleasant memories and storing the last good ones away. All of them were crying for him. That he'd been dragged so suddenly, without a chance to say his last words, without a final goodbye.

What will happen to me, Parina cried. Why aren't these people crying for me? Without my Master, even I'm dead. Who'll clean me, feed me and love me? What about the things I've learnt, trying to fit in here?

The son sensing her sorrow came up and hugged her. He didn't know Parina well enough. But he did know that she was the only other survivor of the old man. And she needed his father more than he did. She was crippled without him—unless…unless they put her back into the sea. But he knew she would hate it.

What the hell, she would be lonely here. Why, even he was feeling orphaned! He might not have had the time for his father but he'd cared. As soon as he realised that he was travelling too frequently, he bought Parina, to entertain his father, to keep him company.

His father had showered the same amount of love on Parina that he'd showered on him as a child. Reading out every book he could lay his shrivelled hands on, patiently teaching her English and feeding her whenever she was hungry. In fact, she'd probably never run out of food during her stay with them. There was always something or the other in the barrel whenever he'd peeped inside.

He wondered how he was going to carry on. He couldn't envisage life without his father. Whenever he thought of life, it glared back with a menacing face as if wanting to seek vengeance for all the cruel comments men and women through the ages had passed on it.

Grumpily, he wondered why life should punish him for others' follies. But life, I guess, has its own track of thoughts, which obviously doesn't coincide with mine, he consoled himself again, now as usual, as he went on with the train of thoughts that life had built for him.

He didn't need anyone in the world more than his father. But now that his father had abandoned him in search of a better life (?), he wondered who would pay attention to his fears when he cried alone in the night? Who would console him in his darkest hour when his experiments failed or blew up in his face? Who would help him out when his theories contradicted themselves and spun around in a loop? Then realising that one could spend one's whole life worrying without fate changing her stubborn mind, he stopped.

A future without his father-friend was something he didn't eagerly look forward to. He was determined not to impose the same fate on the young dolphin. At least he had work to fall back on. She had nothing but yesterday. First thing tomorrow, he would let her go. She's young, she'll make new friends and lead a happy life, a very normal dolphin life, he told himself. Determined, decided, he brushed his lips across her wet mouth, let her go and went back to the coffin.

The dolphin calmed down. The crippling loneliness that had seized her when she first realised that her Master was dead, slackened its grip as the son held her. The warm comforting vibes radiating from his body soothed her tense, uneasy heart. Besides, she realised she wasn't the only one who was lonely. She had company.

Now, she peered at the box intently. The box was being covered with sand. She wanted to scream 'My Master is in that box. Let him out. He isn't dead—he's just having a long nap.' She didn't. She knew he was dead. She was beginning to accept life's swift, silent, cruel end.

After the burial, the Master's son pushed her barrel back home. It was a long walk. But he needed it. He needed to think—straighten his life out.

Tomorrow he would have to let the dolphin go. He couldn't bear watching her distress—she was already pining for his father. Moreover, she would always remind him of his father.

The dolphin sensed something wrong. The Master's son hugged her too often, holding her real tight. Three times in a single day? Parina sensed change. She sensed a new beginning.

At the crack of dawn, the son came into her room with a very early meal. He waited for her to finish and then wheeled her barrel out of the house.

He hated doing this, removing her from her familiar surroundings, but he knew he couldn't look after her. Pushing the barrel was an unenviable, almost uphill task; it kept sinking into the sand. At times, the motor chugged unrelentingly when he increased the accelerator. Sometimes, he had to run to catch up with her. Panting, he still managed to keep a conversation going, to keep her distracted.

He didn't want the happy memories scarred by these last distressful moments. He would rather carry home pictures of her naughty grinning face than this terrified grief-stricken one.

He told her about a slapstick comedy he'd watched, he tried to make her laugh again. Parina listened with other thoughts churning in her mind. When they arrived, the sound of the ocean roared in her head, blasting her mind open. She couldn't help bursting out. 'You are going to throw me into the sea, aren't you?' she asked.

Startled, he hesitated. And then realising that it's meaningless to try to lie to a supersensitive dolphin, he answered in his deep quiet voice, 'Yes, Parina, it's for your own good.' He was a little on the defensive, uncomfortable about abandoning the helpless dolphin.

That's what you say, but what do you know, Parina thought miserably.

'You will be lonely out here,' he rambled on, 'you know I never have the time, I'm either cooped up in my room or I'm attending conferences around the world. Who will look after you, bring you food, love you like father did? Who will give you the care and attention you are so used to?

'You deserve love. Perhaps in your home ground you'll meet another dolphin who'll love you like father did. Maybe more. Wherever you go, just remember that my good wishes are with you. And remember that father is watching over you. Twinkling at you as a star, trying to cheer you up when you're sad and lonely.

'Thanks for bringing so much joy into my father's life. I'll miss you. You've been such an integral part of our lives for such a long time. It's going to be hard to forget you. Love you, take care,' he said, his voice breaking once or twice in between. He then hugged her again, crying shamelessly.

They stayed together that way for a long time. Man and dolphin, clasped in each other's arms, remembering the role the other had played in their brief spell of life together. Remembering the bond they shared—a father.

Parina was the first to break off. Wriggling, she said, 'Actually, I need to thank you for having me in your life. Living with you both, father and son, has been a beautiful experience. The love and affection I've got in your house I might never find elsewhere. Not even in the place where I was born. God bless you with the best that you deserve. I know I'll miss you. Maybe even more than I think I can.' She wondered if she would die heartbroken, sighed and continued.

'Take care. Live life the way you want to. May you never regret your decisions. I doubt your father ever did anything he regretted.'

She stopped suddenly, wondering if her Master had regretted getting her as a surprise gift—the troubles she'd caused, her naughtiness, her selfishness. She wanted to finish before she burst into tears. 'You've taught me a lot. Farewell and take care,' she ended quickly, resigned to fate.

Tears rolled down his cheeks as he stared at her with his frozen anguished face. Admiring her composure, he bid her goodbye. And gently tipped the barrel into the sea.

Parina turned to look at him for one last time, framing a few hurried snapshots of his sweet sensitive face in her mind. With a slow pirouette, she turned and glided away into the deep blue-green sea. She went farther and further away from his searching eyes. Before she slipped over the horizon, a huge wave crashed into her and drowned her beautiful black body.

She had come back to the start. Gone a full circle.

Heart burning like hell on fire, he turned back. Another piece of his life lost forever. He would never see her again. Like he would never see his father. Both detached from his life. Gone forever. One into the

earth and into heaven and the other into the ocean and God knows where.

Life is such. Letting go of loves. If you don't let go, they'll still get snatched away, never to return. But when the eyes are closed and the mind is resting, their spirits will return, haunting as memories. He walked back, to his physics, to his theories, to his experiments, to earning a living, to working for his share of riches in that thirty per cent part of the planet—land.

ALL AT SEA

Even after spending a whole day in the ocean, Parina still felt like a fish out of water. She couldn't understand this world. It's been ages since she'd been exposed to a place where living meant hunting, eating, mating, dying and nothing philosophical.

Everyone was so busy fishing for food, moving restlessly. And the noise! The sea world was worse than a fish market. Everyone talked at once. And it was always something on the lines of 'run, run, run' or 'let's go get him'. Or gestures pointing to such similar topics—surviving. Here they didn't earn a living—they either killed for a living or got killed for someone else's living. Stark and simple.

When she'd left this place, she'd been a baby, too young to think, to form an opinion. But now she was back—older, wiser, an observer. How will I live here for the rest of my life, she wailed. She was already missing her small little barrel. Her quiet, urbane world was so different from this scary, real-life horror show.

She had forgotten what it meant to live here. Ignoring curiosity. Minding your own selfish business. The main worry you ever have in this wild world is how are you going to survive. What are you going to eat? Everything else is irrelevant.

A while back, she had gone and nearly made a fool of herself. While gliding along, hooting at her woe-ridden life, trying not to bask in the warm rays reaching her, she had spied a fish struggling against the transparent fingers of a jellyfish.

Overwhelmed by love, she'd felt extremely sorry for the poor fish. And like a Good Samaritan jumped into the rescue act.

Having decided to aid the poor fish, she rose to collect her breath and plunged in. But lo and behold! The script had changed. The so-called victim's presence had enticed another fish into the tentacles and the jellyfish and the victim (?) were happily gorging on the stunned and stung newcomer.

Shaking her head at their guile, the dolphin had left them alone, grateful that she hadn't bungled in and stirred their emotions.

A great deal of good it would have done them even if they had been angry. I could have easily made a meal of both of them, she thought recklessly. But the next moment, she chided herself for such spiteful thoughts and pulled back into her usual morbid ones.

But in spite of her snobbish attitude towards her new neighbours, she was completely captivated by the world she'd been thrown into. The distinct indifference in the way of life in the watery world made her pause and ponder.

Will I like living this way, she wondered curiously. Then realised, no, she couldn't. She would be bored to death without books, music and television.

She killed time drifting around aimlessly, gulping fish whenever hunger seized her, a sharp eye perpetually on the lookout for other dolphins. She should hang around with her own clan, make new friends, pick up a few basic tips on surviving in the waterworld.

Wandering hither and thither, up north, she stumbled upon a shoal of fish. They were being herded together by a school of dolphins converging on them from all sides. Feeling sorry for the fish, she watched as the dolphins trapped them near the water surface.

Some tried to escape by flying but one or the other predating dolphins manifested out of nowhere to make a meal of the truant fish. After lunch, the school disbanded, each one heading off in a different direction.

Maybe they come together only to feed, she observed. Very organised dining habits. The dolphins had spoken a familiar lingo but she hadn't understood the conversation. She couldn't remember communicating their way.

She hurried to tail a dolphin into dolphin land. But that dolphin wandered around so aimlessly, she gave up after following him around for hours without sighting any place bearing the faintest resemblance to anything like a dolphin land. She didn't want to talk to him though. She was shy and scared. But she wouldn't have minded a crowd. She could've happily been lost in one.

Huh, maybe I'll stumble upon them when I least expect to. Until then, I guess I'll have to bear up with my own company, she thought. But it was getting terribly lonesome. She needed someone to talk to.

PRINCE OF THE WATERWORLD

Once upon a time in the near past, shallow in a mythical, mystical ocean prospered the walrus kingdom. Hundreds of thousands of square feet of land covered with water and studded with oysters and other underwater riches. The king was old, but not yet senile. He loved his wife, his subjects and his colourful, watery country. The only flaw in his otherwise perfect kingdom was his son.

Not the son himself, but rather his attitude towards life. According to his queen and some of his subjects who sometimes inflicted their opinions on him 'out of concern and love', the prince, his son Borick, was out of his mind.

The king's thoughts had been running increasingly jittery over the past few days and always tended to stop at his son, the train of thoughts regularly running on a one-way track.

Borick was not lacking in anything. He was exceedingly handsome, and never before was his kind of bullishness found anywhere in the watery kingdom. Nor was he lacking in the so-called grey matter. The ease with which Borick captured fish sometimes made the poor king feel clumsy and gawky. As a matter of fact, he now ensured that he did his feeding when he was nowhere in the vicinity of his guards.

And as far as riches were concerned, Borick was a prince—an heir at that and nobody in the kingdom could dare him in any display of power and wealth. It must be noted here that riches and power are measured in terms of oysters and mussels, and this grew abundantly in and around the watery palace.

But there is a mutation somewhere. There has to be, no doubt about it. Borick has some very crazy ideas, thought the king, a wee bit sad.

He had come to this sad conclusion after a conversation he had with his son, a few hours back. This conversation had occurred solely on the advice of his queen who enjoyed worrying. In fact, she lived on worries—a heavy diet. If she found nothing to worry about, she would groan and moan like a starved cow.

She wouldn't be happy until someone hunted down some poor unsuspecting worry and brought it home to whine. And her cup of worries always brimmeth over whenever she thought of Borick.

'He is old enough. Ask him to go to land and mate, like everybody else. This season there are plenty of healthy debutantes, so he will breed well. Go, have a talk with him. He should dive at the idea,' she had ordered the king.

Thinking it a very interesting idea but feeling a wee bit shy (such talks the poor king had never had with anyone and no one had ever found it necessary to have one with him), he had looked around for Borick. And finding him teasing a little fish playfully had beckoned him over.

'Son, I need to talk to you,' he said.

'Please do, Dad. You don't require my permission to talk,' Borick retorted. 'And I don't remember you ever asking me for permission whenever you felt like talking. Matter of fact, I have often prayed for silence whenever you get into your talking-to mood,' Borick went on bitterly, remembering all the times he had been pulled up for bad behaviour.

Thick-skinned that he was, the king still sensed Borick's jibe and mumbled reassuringly, 'Son, this is not that kind of a talk. This is a friend-to-friend talk not a father-to-son talk.'

'Okay, so talk! What do you want me to do! Climb a mountain for you?' he asked, his voice dripping with sarcasm. Deep down he didn't want the talk. He sensed something amiss.

But watching his father fidget, he took pity on him and said, 'Okay, Dad. Let's hop onto an iceberg and talk.'

'Sure,' said the king, fidgeting even more. He was not afraid of his son; it was just an embarrassing topic to discuss with him.

'Okay, Dad. Come! Tell me all about it! If you have any problems don't hesitate to share. I have told you as much so many times. I'm glad you've come to me now, though you'll have to hurry and finish it off fast. Arij is waiting at the rookery,' Borick informed his father loftily.

Arij, a seal, was Borick's best friend.

'It's all right then, you carry on! This can wait,' the king said, hoping Borick would take the hint and disappear. Then he would dive into the icy water and cool his cheeks which were burning like the good old sun on a midsummer noon.

'No, Dad. Arij can wait. He'll wait. Otherwise, I'll go to his place and meet him there. No, no! You tell me what you came to say. Come on, let's get it over and done with.'

I know my son is very understanding. I know him very well. Borick is a rare gem, the like of which has never dazzled in this world and will never dazzle again. He's one in a million, is my son Borick, the king told himself trying to encourage himself to have the conversation.

Father and son climbed onto an iceberg, nearly toppling it. It was a huge one, very sturdy. And it could easily bear their combined weight without a whimper. Although at times it nearly sank it revived again. Shuffling, to make themselves comfortable, they tested its strength further. It put up with them patiently, like a grandpa giving a piggyback ride to his little wriggling ones.

'Son, it is so quiet here.'

Quietness and serenity were currently as rampant as corals on icebergs. Borick wondered if his father was deaf. Even the deaf would have heard the seagulls shrieking their guts out but dad was obviously lost in thought or perhaps was just oblivious to the world around him.

After much fidgeting and shuffling, his father began and went on, 'Your mother was saying...' Borick wondered what his mother had said and tried to keep his mind from wandering.

'So, my son, it is time you mated,' the king ended quickly, a messenger now resigned to his impending execution.

So, this is what it's all about, Borick spat in his mind. Mama thinks I'm old enough, so I should mate like all normal walruses. No wonder dad was so nervous. This is definitely the first time we've had such a talk. Poor father… sent to coax me into abiding with my queen mother's wishes.

Even as the king waited for a reply, Borick wondered what his father would say if he voiced his opinion about their pathetic way of life. Would he get angry, and disinherit and exile him? Or would he try to wriggle out of the delicate topic? Most likely he would try to convince him about the way a walrus ought to live: eat-mate-die. Still, he felt like giving it a try.

'Dad, listen carefully. I am not going to repeat this. The next time you make me repeat this, I'll leave this kingdom and you'll never see me again. So better clean your ears and listen up,' Borick began.

'My idea of life is different. And I'm going to live my life the way I want to. I do not want to mate with just any female who thinks I will sire healthy babies. No, sir. What I want is a cow I can love—one who'll understand my mind. A female I can respect. I don't want to mate just to have babies and increase our hoard. If I ever mate, I will do it with my perfect match.

'It sounds crazy but I think I'm capable of finding my own life mate,' he ended. He said all this slowly, spelling out each syllable so his father wouldn't lose his mind and thunder. He also paused after each word waiting for the meaning to sink in before continuing.

To his credit, the king wasn't angry. He was astounded.

Whoever heard of love in the watery kingdom, in the walrus kingdom! This was a first. And coming out of his own baby's mouth! He was shocked.

The king in his own vagrant, younger years had heard of swans pining away, dolphins and whales too. Personally, he was of the opinion that love is a very foolish and useless emotion.

A bit unnerved by his son's manner of thoughts, he had tried, really tried, to din into his head, the dangers of falling into love. Love can only bring sorrow, he warned. He himself had seen some lonely souls pining away for their lost loves and that wonderful bit of experience was not what the old king wished upon his young, sensitive son.

What I call love extends to even the fish I eat, but Borick's seems to be on an entirely different level altogether, he sighed, wondering why his son hadn't grown up to be more like him.

'But son,' he tried once more.

'No buts, Dad,' Borick had butted in. 'I'm going to do just what I want to do. And what I want to do is find my love and I'm going to find her.' With that, he had jumped into the ocean and gone in search of Arij.

The king had stayed there for a long time, feeling sorry for Borick. When you aim high and fall short, unless you have the ability to bounce back, you're bound to break. And he didn't want a battered, broken son. It's better not to jump when you know you'll fall and get hurt.

Shaking his head, the king had returned to his peaceful haven where everything jumped to attention when he spoke and cautiously steered clear of his queen. He knew he was a failure and was in no mood to listen to the degree to which he was a failure—something he was sure his queen would've happily acquainted him with.

SOUL TALK

Growling angrily under his breath, Borick had set off in search of Arij and found him midway to the rookery.

Tired of waiting, Arij was plodding his way back home.

'Why late?' asked Arij, then noticed the wild, staring eyes, the flushed cheeks and instantly regretted his question. Sparks flew when Borick was angry. And today he was soaring like the eagles touching the sun.

'It's my dad! He wants me to mate,' Borick spluttered.

'Oh?' Arij murmured, scared to speak further. He fidgeted, he knew a sensitive spot when he saw one and this was visibly raw, freshly bruised.

'Mother knows my views on this issue and has still badgered my dad into talking to me,' he explained, turning his temper knob higher.

'Why can't she leave me alone?' he snarled. Diving into the shallow waters, he angrily dug out a mollusc and sucked on it noisily.

'She is worried, Borick. You're her only son and a prince at that,' Arij ventured mildly.

'Worried? Is that something new? When isn't she worried? She would worry if her hair grew a hair's breadth longer than usual. Wonder how dad puts up with her!'

'Race you to the rookery,' Arij called out, reluctant to spoil his own sunny mood. In a trice, he had bounded away with half a whale's lead.

In no mood for such frivolous activities, Borick plodded along at his own pace. Hauling himself out of the water, he soaked in the sun, grumbling and wishing that he had found someone who could make him happy.

He felt foolish talking of love and the like. But he desperately wanted to love, wanted to feel love, desire, life. He was dying to feel the pain, the bittersweet joy that love is supposedly so generous with. He sat there, wondering if love exists, whether his lover is somewhere, lonely, waiting for him... Wondering if he'll meet her, when? He hoped he will, soon, and sent out a silent prayer.

The walrus and the seal were quiet for a long time, unwilling to intrude on the other's thoughts. Arij amused himself with the waves, drifting, sailing, then flipping and turning against them. But he was sad, very sad.

Borick pivoted suddenly to face him. 'Arij! When will I find her?' he asked softly, struggling to keep the fear of loneliness out of his voice.

Arij got out of the water, shuffled up to him and raised his soft, gentle eyes. He knew this feeling and sympathised. He knew there was such a thing called love. He himself was in love. Agreed, he had made plenty of mistakes, ridden all the wrong currents, but in the end he'd found what he had been looking for—his own sweet Cutra.

He knew he could have easily been lost, searching for love in the ocean of life. The temptations that lead love can guide you to death. The more you fight it, the deeper you get sucked in. Love is like quicksand. When trapped, stay calm. Do not resist. And help itself comes in search of you.

He had been lucky. He had waited and allowed destiny to guide him in his tricky life. Soon, he'd been bored of the imitations and learnt to be choosy. And then at last, he had found his Cutra and had never had any problems whatsoever. She was for life, but what a lot of time he'd spent waiting for her. Of course, he understood the fears, the apprehensions invading Borick's mind. He too had trudged up the same lonely, scary path.

Trying to throw his black mood, Borick turned and asked, 'So how is your famous romance going? Everything fine? Cutra seems to have brought a new sheen to your already shining body.'

That was a usual one. Borick always teased Arij about his shining, slimy body and Arij always bantered back about the walrus's own wrinkled skin. He could still remember the first time he'd met Borick. Arij was being chased by a huge walrus. It was a life-and-death situation. Resigned to death, he had slowed down after having dodged the monster successfully for over three hundred miles.

Any moment now, I will be battered and crushed into pieces on a rock, he'd thought.

The walrus had caught him but had immediately let go. Arij had turned back and seen his captor being shoved aside by another walrus.

He had immediately felt sorry for his captor. After all, he'd caught him after a tiring chase. And it was extremely mean of the newcomer to take advantage of someone else's prize, he had decided, and had been tempted to help his captor fight the newcomer away.

But before he'd embarked on his foolhardy task, his survival instincts got the better of his sense of fairness and he had made good his escape. However, unable to resist a backward glance, he had sneaked a look and had seen his captor slinking away defeated and dejected.

The newcomer had sauntered off in the opposite direction. Feeling terribly grateful, Arij had swum to the safety of his home, wondering about his rescuer.

Now, looking at Borick, he couldn't believe they'd met just a year back. He felt like he'd known him all his life.

He hadn't seen him immediately after the rescue act, he remembered. He had deliberately hung around in that dangerous territory hoping to catch sight of

Borick to convey his gratitude, though he probably ought to have said 'sorry' and not 'thanks' for jumping to such horrible conclusions. But he hadn't seen him for over a week.

But then one day, while sunning himself, he had spied a walrus on a lonely, isolated iceberg. Wondering if it was his rescuer, he had slipped off and moved closer to the other thin slab of ice.

When he got closer, he recognised his rescuer. And promptly, his brain played dead.

Heart pounding, he had mustered up courage from all the crevices in his body. Goading himself to complete the task he had embarked upon, he had climbed onto the iceberg and wriggled towards the walrus.

Then clearing his throat he had waited, sure that the walrus would hear and turn. But no! The walrus had shown no sign of having heard his approach. Maintaining his composure intact, assuming a very respectful stance, Arij had begun with a 'Sir?' The walrus turned and looked at him for a couple of seconds and turned back and continued gazing at the gulls.

Encouraged by the slight movement, which told him that he was indeed being heard, he took a deep breath and began pouring his heart out.

'Sir, thanks! Thanks for rescuing me that day. I know it was none of your concern. You could have just left me to die. But kind-hearted that you are, you rescued me. Thank you, sir. I am genuinely grateful to you. Indebted. Thank you, so much, sir. Without your help that day, I wouldn't have seen the sun today. I've been looking out for you all these days but I couldn't find you. Now, that I have found you, I thank...'

He would have gone on for another hour if the walrus, sickened by the amount of thanks being heaped on him, hadn't growled.

Startled, Arij had jumped, and in the process fallen head on into the water and surfaced spluttering.

It was then that he heard the guffaw. Laughter rolling like thunder. The iceberg shook indecisively. To drown or not to drown was the million-pearl question. Arij looked up to see the walrus shaking with uncontrollable mirth.

Thoroughly irritated, he had rocked the iceberg. And the ocean rose to welcome the mighty walrus.

The walrus recovered from his clumsy fall and swam up to him. Heart fluttering, underside perspiring, Arij waited for the fatal strike. But the walrus had smiled. 'Let's be friends,' he'd said, adding, 'I'm Borick.'

And they had been friends ever since. Small footsteps towards respect and love helped their friendship go a long way.

Snapping out of his reverie, Arij saw Borick peering at him like he was a creature from another ocean. 'What are you looking at me like that for?' Arij asked, flustered.

'What were you thinking of now? You seemed to have shuttled off to some other waters.'

'Just remembering the last one year.'

'Last one year? Why?'

'It's been a year since we met.'

'Just a year. It seems like ages.'

'Yeah, I know. Even I feel the same.'

'Yeah?'

'Umm...'

'You haven't answered my question, how's Cutra?'

'Fine. She sent her regards.'

'You should've brought her along.'

Arij hesitated. 'Well, she was busy.'

'Busy? Doing what? Playing chase with the other seals, uh?'

Arij kept mum.

'She's forever playing, isn't she?' he drawled, interpreting the silence for a reluctant 'yes'.

'Maybe. But she's a sweetheart and makes me feel good.'

'Selfish,' Borick chided.

'Huh, who isn't?' Arij countered, his eyes serious.

Selfishness is not a sin, if it is then each one of us is a sinner, Borick heard someone say. The voice was soft and gentle and sounded quite wise. He looked around but there wasn't a soul. And it definitely wasn't Arij's voice. He would have known.

CUPID STRIKES!

The sun was fast vacating post, disappearing to his home in his faraway continent, pulling his golden robes after him. The sky was blushing burgundy, yet to recover from his warm, fulfilling presence.

Arij and Borick gaped at the heavenly show from their high podium, the ice floe. They watched as the scene changed, patiently waiting for the new actors to appear and play their parts. They watched the never-ending, ever-refreshing show, frozen as statues, afraid to move, lest they disturb the stars, make them fumble and fall out of the fast darkening, gloomy-eyed sky.

Borick had wanted to climb a rock for a better view, but Arij had managed to dissuade him from the adventurous task and recommended the ice floe. He now stole glances at Borick and asked, 'What are you looking for, Borick?'

Borick knew where Arij's mind had stalled. 'I don't know,' he replied.

'A beautiful, healthy cow with brains, right?' Arij asked knowingly.

'I really don't know. I have seen many maidens, some even warm and furry, but somehow nobody seems right. I can't get close.'

'With a hide like yours even the craggiest mountain would envy you,' Arij piped in.

'"Rugged" is the word,' Borick said absentmindedly. In his clan, thick skin was a gift of longevity.

'And, of course, they're healthy, they would've borne fine heirs but I never felt they were for me,' Borick continued.

'Then what are you looking for?' Arij asked, knowing the answer.

'Like I said, I don't know,' he pursed his lips. 'Maybe when I find her, I will know.'

'Fat chance you have of finding something you don't even know you want,' Arij remarked.

'You know, somehow I think I'll kind of stumble upon her. One day when the sky is blue, no clouds marring her complexion and the sun is bright and sunny, I'll spot a beautiful maiden reclining on an iceberg. Entranced by her beauty, I'll move closer, our eyes will meet and then my whole world will spin faster—all signs of a great event unfolding! I will recognise her as the star of my dreams. Something similar will happen to her and she too will realise that I'm the one she's born for. Then both of us will dive into love and the world will turn into a beautiful early morning dream. All of us live happily ever after! How's that?' Borick drawled dreamily, his face flushed.

'Huh! Keep dreaming! It might just turn out that way!' said Arij.

Both of them turned to watch the stars, retreating into their own minds. Borick with a blissful smile plastered on his face, dreaming of love and happiness, and Arij remembering the pain and unhappiness that follows at times.

Arij had a foreboding that some disaster was about to strike and he was terribly worried. Borick had his head in the clouds and was paddling into trouble blindly.

'I'm hungry. Come, let's dig out some molluscs,' he heard Borick say.

A black ballistic missile whizzed past them, neatly splitting the ocean. Arij was stunned. 'Wow, what a beauty!' he breathed unconsciously.

'Arij...' Borick threatened, a steel wire framing his voice.

'Okay, okay, I'm sorry,' Arij apologised without thinking, and then burst out. 'Hey! Why don't you dig up your molluscs yourself? It's easy for you with your tusks. When I try, my nose always gets scraped! No, no! Dig them up yourself, I'm not going to do it!'

'And pray, what will you do while I dig? Admire flamboyant dolphins, no doubt?' Borick asked dryly and then added, 'No, Arij! Either you feed me or off you go to get Cutra,' all the while trying to steal surreptitious glances at the dolphin.

'You can't force me!' Arij cried, alloying some steel into his voice. Involuntarily, he took a step back in fear, forgetting his friendship.

Suddenly Borick froze. A strange fire lit up his eyes as he stared at the dolphin.

Then abruptly, his body relaxed, as if he'd melted. Slowly and very deliberately, he said, 'Arij, I think I've found her. She is just what I've been looking for!'

'What!?! What are you talking about?' Arij gasped, flabbergasted, though he knew what Borick meant.

'My love. She's the one.'

'That dolphin? What's wrong with you?'

'Dolphin? Oh yes, she's a dolphin. But so what?'

'She's a dolphin and that's what,' Arij reminded him angrily. 'How can you a walrus call a dolphin your soulmate? I know you're out of your mind, but this is ridiculous,' he muttered in disgust.

'Arij! Just shut up.'

'Yeah, sure, but when things go wrong, don't tell me that I didn't warn you!'

'If that day comes...'

'It will, you just wait,' Arij was shaking his head vigorously, not allowing any thoughts to settle in his head.

'Arij! Shut up,' Borick growled as he swam towards the dolphin. Bowing to her, he said, 'Prince Borick at your service, Ma'am.'

The dolphin just stared at him. She then said something, squawking rapidly. Borick gaped, not understanding a word. Some other language! God, I needed this, he thought, exasperated.

Thrusting his chin into his neck, 'Borick, Borick,' he repeated.

Her eyes gleamed with understanding. 'Borick?' she asked.

The walrus nodded encouragingly. 'Borick,' he repeated, staring into her eyes.

'Borick?' she asked, in amazement. The walrus was looking at her expectantly. 'Parina,' she said in answer.

'Pai-a,' he said, rock in his mouth.

'Parina,' she said, rebuking him.

'Paria,' he insisted, stubbornly.

'Parina,' she corrected gently.

'Paina,' he growled, not interested in prolonging this introduction any further.

He then gestured for her to follow him and swam to his abode. Arij waited for a while and quickly caught up with them. He didn't say a word, it would have been too dangerous! When Borick got angry, his face got all screwed up, ready to explode. One wrong word and hell would break loose. Borick was an absolute terror if his temper was ignited.

Borick lived on top of a mossy sea mountain. He preferred this to his father's luxurious oyster-studded palace. He liked it because it was soft and comfortable. Parina fell in love with it because it was green and reminded her of land. And, anyway, he needn't have asked her twice. She would have gladly jumped through a burning hoop if he'd so desired.

Without any formal discussions, they decided to live together.

Arij hung around for a while, watching Borick serenade the dolphin.

The dolphin was laughing and encouraging Borick who was lapping up her attention with a silly smile plastered on his face. After a long time, not interested in being a silent spectator to Borick making a complete fool of himself, Arij mumbled his goodbye. The dolphin looked up and gave him a shy smile and squawked a goodbye.

Plodding his way back home, Arij tried to shake off the warning bells ringing in his head. He foresaw violent whirlpools, horrifying hurricanes and thunderbolts striking. He was troubled.

But fate is not something a mere mortal can tamper with. Whatever has to happen will happen, he thought, and tried to convince himself that he was helpless.

HOME AGAIN

It wasn't that she didn't know the language, she had forgotten it, that's all. Long time, no withdrawal had shelved her native tongue into a frozen account and the memory bank had shifted to a new address.

Once, ages ago, her Master had dropped a couple of goldfish into her barrel, warning her not to eat them. So she ended up getting friendly with them instead.

Cheeky little devils, she remembered now, always nibbling at her fins or her tail. It had tickled her into laughter, but laughter's so terribly distracting when you're trying to trap a fish. Her meal would invariably escape when she chortled. She would then chase the goldfish all over the barrel, threatening murder if she caught them. But they always eluded her, slipping under her so she couldn't catch them!

But they had been a cheerful pair. Together they had some really great times. They would regale her with hilarious episodes from the waterworld, she remembered.

She knew the language, she'd lost track of it, that's all. Maybe if I concentrate and dig hard enough, I can salvage words and phrases, she thought now and searched for her old memory bank.

Excited, she hunted around for Borick and said, 'Talk to me.' Borick didn't understand what she said, but eventually got the hang of her human inflection and taught her the underwater language.

Within a few days, she could speak as well as him. Talking, of course, didn't head Borick's list of pastimes. He spoke only when necessary or when he was forced to answer. It was enough for her to learn. Soon, she began to try out her newly restored language on him and Arij.

Arij suffered her gladly. In the beginning, he had stayed aloof, not talking, not sharing in their jokes and laughter but gradually he had given up his stuffiness and had grown to love the showy, attention-seeking, but lovable dolphin.

Soon they began spending long hours together discussing the unpredictability of life. Arij shyly confided in Parina about Cutra and she told him about her Master. Gradually a bond developed and pulled them closer, until Arij began spending nearly all his waking hours with Parina. He never brought Cutra along, though he did point her out once to Parina when she was playing with her friends.

Borick never left Parina's side, but he never voiced his thoughts either, preferring to be a reserved yet attentive observer.

Despite being the recipient of single-minded devotion and love from the two handsome males, Parina was sometimes sucked into the whirlpool of despair. Whenever she thought of her Master, she felt lonely, deserted and abandoned. She missed her previous life. She cried for her yesterday; she missed the fun she used to have.

She longed to hear the stories from the Bible again. She yearned to learn more about Shambala. She was dying to hear her Master read aloud his son's books. Her Master's son was a reputed physicist. Her Master had spent hours reading aloud the huge books he sent home sometimes. As a result, Parina had been hooked on the profound probabilities of quantum mechanics. Here in this mundane world she missed that thirsty quest, the adventure of science.

If I was a human being, I would have figured out the secrets of this universe, of laughter, of sorrow! I would have tried, she often thought. The more she yearned, the more she realised that it was a hopeless dream. Her dream to be Man.

Borick sensed her secret desires but could do nothing about it. All he could do was encourage her to relive her past by talking about Man's world, and that he did. Instantly cheered, she would rattle off by the dozen, telling him all that she could think of.

She told him about the man with the small moustache—the one who had massacred thousands just because he didn't like their religion, the one who had tried to wipe out an entire race of humans by gassing them in torture chambers.

She told him about the half-naked man with the stick and the cute glasses—the one who had starved for over a month to stop people from killing each other for their religious beliefs, but for all his peace-making efforts, ate a bullet and died. She then needed to explain what a bullet was. Her stories never ended, every sentence starting a new story.

Once in a way, a passing fish would stop to listen to her tales, wondering whether such a world really existed. Seeing the fish listening agog, some of his friends would stop and so it happened that whenever Parina talked there was a huge crowd. The audience listened eagerly, lapping up all the strange happenings in Man's world. They would also ask her questions at times, eager to know what happened to their family and friends when they were caught by Man. However, Parina encouraged no questions.

She insisted that she would tell them only those things she wanted to talk about and not a word more. In the beginning they were irritated, terribly dissatisfied, then realising that it's useless to badger her into doing something she didn't want to do, finally resigned themselves to listening to whatever she doled out.

Parina revelled in this uncalled-for attention. No more was she lonely. She talked and talked, preaching about the good and the bad. She told them everything she had learnt when living with Man.

Parina through her stories made the school cry. She also made them smile. She made her presence felt. She made them feel, she strummed on their heartstrings. Her audience loved her, they wanted encores. Whenever she started talking, word passed around, and that day, they all gathered around.

After some initial disturbances, a rule was imposed. When she preached, no one was supposed to prey. This was so that even the lesser creatures could listen without fear, in peace, and also to avoid commotion and disarray.

But for all her attention-seeking ways, Parina was not an ingrate. In spite of such a wide audience, she continued to be faithful to Borick and Arij, her first friends, and always sought out their company after her talks. They were special.

She made sure she kept aside some things especially for them, what she considered juicy and was sentimental about. She told them about the romantic poets, about Lucy Gray who dwelt among the untrodden ways. She sang the songs of innocence and experience. She lingered over the trials of Psyche and Cupid. She explained the rules of physics, she deliberated on metaphysics. She did not delve deep into the idea of God though. Both Arij and Borick had their own different Gods, pictured in the perfect form of their own species. She did not want to argue or question their beliefs. Everyone has their own Gods, she knew. She didn't want to be sacrilegious. God is God, whatever form He assumes.

The three of them agreed on two things however. One was that there is a reason for life, to continue living—a sort of a quest for treasure. The description of the treasure was the bone of contention.

Borick believed that life is a quest for love and the emotions it inspires. Arij believed life to be a quest for innocence, the simple joy of living, playing, loving. Parina's idea was inspired by her previous life on land. She believed life is a quest for knowledge. Knowledge about anything remotely connected to life, from the beginning to the end. That is why she loved science. It explained life on earth, precisely, in measurable terms.

The other thing they agreed and healthily disagreed upon was love. Borick felt love has to be trapped, or would otherwise neatly glide out of one's life, never to appear again. Arij on his part believed that there is just one love and that love exists for the only reason of being loved and hence would always surface at the right time.

Now Parina did not believe in any such sentimental nonsense. Love for her was a basic necessity. Love was comforting when lonely, a confidante for the fears that wrench the heart, a light on a moonless night.

Love always surfaces at all places, at all times. Love changes, loves change. Love flies and love dies. Yesterday her master had been her love. Today Borick was her love. And if he isn't around tomorrow, she would always find someone as loving as him, is what she believed. No dearth of love. As long as you want to love, you'll find a worthy lover. You just need to look around and meet someone's eyes, she knew. But she didn't voice her thoughts aloud, reluctant to hurt Borick, who she knew was obsessed with her. So she preferred silence when love's debates flared.

Nevertheless the three friends had some roaring discussions on various other topics too, sometimes well into the deep dark night. And they always went back satisfied, lighter, with no hard feelings driving a wedge between them.

LOVE SUCKS!

A week had flown by since Parina had been thrown into this world. She was dying to speak in English. Once in a while, she tried to teach the walrus some English, to entertain herself. She saw a shoal of fish peacefully passing by. Trapping one and keeping it protruding out of her mouth, she nodded towards it, and looked at the prince.

'Fish,' she said, as the fish fell out and escaped. 'That fish.'

The walrus just looked at her puzzled. 'Aaah?' he moaned and shifted uneasily. What is this cow up to, he wondered.

He didn't understand a word. But letting her know that would be a mistake. So he just nodded and tried repeating it. 'Thah fuss,' he tried.

The dolphin sensed the defiance beneath the façade of impenetrable calm yet persisting, repeated, 'That, fish.'

'Thas fess,' he tried again.

Taking pity on the walrus, she trapped another one, gulped it down, eyes fixed on the walrus throughout and said, 'This fish my food.'

'Tah fuss my fuss,' he answered.

Smiling at that, Parina repeated again, 'This fish… my food.'

Stung by the smile, Borick flapped his flippers belligerently and with a violent splash hauled himself onto a chunk of ice to cool his temper. 'Infuriating cow!' he snarled. 'Always teasing me! There has to be a limit.'

Parina also surfaced. She traced an imaginary arc in the air. She leapt up and took a neat dive, shooting into the water like a torpedo.

Borick ignored her. He tried not to admire her beauty.

Holding her breath, Parina glided stealthily to the tip of the iceberg, and bumped into it at its most vulnerable place, heaving. The iceberg rose and threw the unwary walrus into the sea.

SPLASH! He fell clumsily. Thoroughly annoyed now, the walrus growled menacingly.

Undeterred by this pretence of anger, Parina slowly glided up to him, rubbed him with her flippers and said, 'Love.'

This language he understood, of course. Overwhelmed with tender feelings, he just stared at her wondering at her patience in bearing up with his slowness. He knew how badly she wanted to teach him Man's language, how desperate she was to share her past with him. But the language of Man was a stumbling block, consisting of mouthfuls of rocky, rounded words. Normally, she taught him English through their common underwater language. But today... 'Rrooo' he growled in pain.

Parina had bit him on his chest, hard.

'Ouuu foolus cow!' he roared in fake anger and chased her. But she was too quick for him. She somersaulted, spinning circles in space, bouncing into the water, shooting out like a malleable missile, her elastic body curving, bending like a bow, piercing the ocean like an arrow...

'Oops!' The walrus had waited and had moved suddenly and her beautiful black body hit the rock-like one. Her jaw nearly broke. Laughing, the prince rubbed against her flippers, lovingly tickling her with his whiskers.

'My love! What am I going to do with you? Half the time you irritate me and the other half you bowl me over with your beauty.'

Parina shuffled, cut loose and swam across towards the sea mountain. She didn't like it when the walrus oozed mush. It made her terribly uneasy. A voice inside chastened her for taking more than she was ready to give. Eager to split before he turned into jelly, she asked him to follow and glided away.

GOOD LORD!

'Oh Lord! What do we do now?' someone wailed. 'Were you blind or what? Missing our God?'

'Stupid whale.'

'All blubber, no brain.'

'Stop it! What do you gain by insulting him? What's done is done! Let's think of a way to appease the Almighty.'

'Yes, yes,' they agreed in unison.

'He'll send a fire. He'll poison the water and choke us,' someone voiced his fear.

'Nonsense! There is no such fire. How do you manage to dream up such gory things?'

'No, no! My cousin has seen that fire! It burnt the water and the smoke rose to the heavens, the clouds were black for months after,' someone put in.

'Maybe... I don't know.'

'Anyway, what do we do now to pacify Him?'

'Look, there's Parina! Let's ask her!'

'Parina!'

She turned, saw the crowd and the hovering gloom and quickly glided towards them.

'What happened?' Parina asked in surprise. She looked around and saw the whale at the centre of the crowd. The whale was grinning sheepishly. He had blundered, he knew. But he hadn't done it deliberately. And any God would surely forgive an accident if He was as good as they said he was.

But this crowd of puny little fish have seized the opportunity and are raining insults! As though I had connived and plotted to knock the place down just to spite them. Stupid creatures! I can gobble the whole shoal in one gulp he thought, his temper soaring.

However the whale wasn't the vengeance wrecking kind. He killed out of hunger and not in anger. So before the minute was up, he had chided himself for his wicked thought.

Right now, he was a trifle amused by the righteous anger of these tiny fish. He knew that if he'd done it to his own God he would have had some scars to show for it. His fellow creatures would have thrashed him around and probably chewed his flippers out. The thought left him grave and he looked at Parina curiously.

He had heard of her but had never set his eyes on her, never bothered to. This was the first time he was checking her out.

The whale's jaw dropped. Jeez, he nearly exclaimed aloud, his eyes popping out of their holes. The lady was gorgeous. Then recovering, he grinned sheepishly again, a little embarrassed by his star-struck behaviour.

Parina swept him with a dismissing glance and turned back to the crowd. An elderly fish explained the situation to her. 'This whale has knocked our shrine down. He says it was an accident. We know it's true, but accident or no accident God will get angry. And we're terribly scared... terrified of the Mighty One's wrath!'

'Parina, tell us what to do? Help us, Parina. Please?' a fish begged.

Parina looked at the toppled rock and then at the fish around her. Looking each one in the eye, she said slowly, 'God is not only in this stone you worship.'

Everyone perked up. Good! One more lecture, they thought, and waited to lap it up.

'He is in you—in me—in this fish—in his neighbour—in your neighbour—everywhere. He is everywhere, not trapped in this stone alone.'

'But, Parina, our fathers and forefathers have been worshipping this for ages,' someone protested.

'Then whom do we worship? Ourselves?' someone asked.

Someone else chortled.

Parina sought the offender out and withered him with a glance. 'If you don't have the Devil in you, then fine, go ahead and worship yourself. There's nothing wrong in that,' she said and continued slowly, softly, casting her spell...

'There is no heaven or hell where you perceive it to be. Your own body is heaven or hell, by your own choice. The goodness in you indicates the presence of God, evil the Devil's. They have both lodged themselves inside you, constantly at war, battling for power over your soul, tearing you apart.

'It is entirely your choice, whom you want to worship. If you wish to live in peace, throw the Devil out. Expel the evil in you. Even its scent makes God restless. Work towards being good and you pay homage to the God residing in you.

'God is nowhere else, but in you, in me, in my neighbours, in yours, in that stone, in that plankton. He is the goodness in everyone. Worship that. Abhor the evil in the person.

'Do not turn him away because he is bad, because he is helping the Devil. Help him overpower the Devil in him. Help him allow God to reside in him. Pity him, because the Devil in him will be the cause of his ruin. No one can allow the Devil sole presence in his soul. If he has, then he's already on his way to damnation and hell. Nothing can save him from his gruesome fate, unless he is kind to himself and good to other souls. Then, perhaps, God will have mercy and try to save him.

'You have to strengthen God by your innate goodness. Such is the power of your soul. Even God needs your help. And God is essentially goodness. Be good. Be kind to everyone. Do not kill in anger. Do not hurt anybody whatever their faults.

'And do not worry about something as trivial as knocking a stone down. All that the whale has done is to offend the belief of your ancestors by desecrating this place. By now, they too would have realised the stupidity of worshipping stones. There is no point in worshipping stones or any such godly icons, if you are going to go on a rampage, kill in anger, act like the Devil. Stop. Search. Seek out the goodness in you and pray for everyone. Forgive and love every creature,' she concluded.

The school of fish listened intently, searching for flaws to prove her wrong. How can all creatures have God in them and be so powerful, they wondered. But they were quite blind to the holes in her speech, if any, so gulped it down eagerly.

The novelty of the whole idea pushed them onto a new path, gave them a different approach to life. They were searching for something new, something different from their timeworn beaten path, the one they had followed generation after generation without questioning.

However Borick turned away, very disturbed. If there is such a thing as God in everyone, then how many Gods are living in this world, he wondered.

What happens to Him when the creature dies? Does He die too? How many Gods have I killed and eaten?

Is life just an accident, or is there any specific reason for living? Why are we here? How did we happen, he wondered. He meditated on the questions but came up with no answers. Next he put forth his questions to Parina.

But she hedged and tried to evade answering, unwilling to admit her own lack of knowledge. Parina preached whatever little she knew, whatever she remembered from the books her Master had read out to her. Beyond that, she couldn't think on her own.

Frustrated, Borick sought seclusion. He spent the entire evening on an iceberg, searching the sky. Finding no answers there, he withdrew within himself. He ignored Parina for the rest of the day.

Borick spent a sleepless night and woke up more restless than usual. He was seized by an overwhelming urge to climb the nearest mountain to get closer to God. He had tried before, but had never been able to scale it to the top. But today, the urge seemed to be pumping power into his already willing body.

He was absolutely determined to climb up to the snow-capped peak to look down on the beautiful world. He wanted to know how the world was created. Perhaps, through His work I'll know Him, he thought.

He trudged towards the mountain double-checking the frost-covered rocks he put his flippers on, careful not to tumble down.

It wasn't a steep mountain. More like a hillock, dressed in snow-white rocks and boulders, and not difficult to mount at all. The mountain's snowy face shielded him from the sun's cloudy rays. The only stumbling block was the height. The walrus was exhausted even before he'd started.

Slowly and surely, he climbed, not wanting to cause himself any injury. Injury meant sure death in his sea kingdom and he didn't want to die young. Even a bruise can be fatal, enough to get the sharks on your trail. Survival of the fittest is the order of the day, every day, in his watery world. His preoccupation with being unduly careful took up all the space in his mind. Restlessness stopped rearing its tiring head. Mind clear of all tiresome thoughts, concentrating on just surviving, he climbed on.

Noon flew past and the sun was getting dressed for his evening party. The wind raged furiously threatening to knock him off his feet. But Borick was a sturdy rock, he couldn't be blown away so easily. By the time he had climbed three-fourth of the way, he thought he would die of exhaustion. But he clung to his life and pushed ahead.

'I can do it,' he muttered fiercely, as he shoved himself on.

At last, there was just a yard to the top. All he had to do was follow the path between the snowy rocks and he would be perched on the peak. All through the trek, he had fixed his eyes on the treacherous terrain. Not once had he looked around. He was dying to see the world from the mountain top. He wanted to look down on the world. Feel like God!

Eagerness spouted a sudden spring in his flippers, and he hopped on ahead.

Finally, completely exhausted, he reached the summit. Taking a deep breath, he looked down at the raging beauty of the ocean. Water, water, restless, moving water everywhere. Whales lashing their forked tails, restless. Fish jumping, restless. Only the birds seemed peaceful. And why not? They could fly! The wind tried to push them around. But they used the wind to sail, retaining their grace and course.

Perhaps, sensing his desire to be alone, they hadn't come anywhere near his mountain. He looked beyond the waters, to see where the world ended. He could see nothing but a thin line separating the ocean from the sky. He could see no further.

He saw the sun, the red ball of fire, dropping and dipping into the sea. He waited for it to sink. He half-expected a sizzle and mist to rise out. But no, without a sound, the sun disappeared inch by inch into the water, sorely tempting Borick to dive in to rescue it.

He watched as the sky blushed and then turned dark. Remembering that he had a long trek back, he envied the birds that had now flown away. They could come here with a flick of their wings. They don't need a mountain to cling to. They soar up into the skies and look down on the world. They climb upto heaven and act like the messengers of God.

But they can't dive into the deep sea, to mother earth's womb, he consoled himself. Where does God live, he now wondered. Up in the sky or down in the ocean?

Again, the familiar restlessness reared its ugly head and he let loose his thoughts. So far above the ground, he somehow felt closer to heaven, felt the potent presence of God, could see his work and appreciate him better.

Searching the black sky, he found a star and asked, 'What is behind all this? Why am I here? Why is the sun here? Why are you here? Where did we come from? How did it all happen? Is there a God? Hey, God? Are you alive? Can I see Your Face?'

There was no answer. He shouted out the questions again and waited.

Again, no reply. Of course, there's no God. He is just a figment of our imagination. We need a scapegoat, so we create a God and curse Him or worship Him. All depending on the way our day turns out, he thought, completely disillusioned. Or maybe, He thinks I'm not worthy of an answer.

Stung by this blank, no-reply line he'd connected to after such a taxing day, he lurched, his mind deranged. All of a sudden, thunder roared and lightning streaked in the sky, as if God was furious with his behaviour and was about to strike him dead.

Borick blacked out.

He could see nothing, feel nothing. Somewhere in the distance, in a faraway continent, a light flickered.

He tried to inch closer, grab it with his mind, touch it, hold it, inflame it, rouse it into a bonfire. The flame flared, spread its fingers, licked him and consumed him entirely. He exploded back into life, bursting with joy. He knew it. He knew his past and his future. Images of elephants, lions, tigers, men, aliens, all the forms—all the bodies he'd lived through—catwalked across his mind.

He knew why he was in this world. He was here to help, to help himself and everyone else. To spread the light, to erase darkness, to spread happiness, and to erase pain.

God is not only in a stone, he is in everyone, whispered a voice in his mind. Yes, Parina was right. Man is right, to a great extent. Though Man himself doesn't actually believe in the power of his own thoughts.

A serene, mystical look invaded Borick's face. His eyes shone with the fire of conviction. Instead of trudging back, he closed his eyes and materialised in the ocean. Making his easy way back home, he was finally at peace.

SERMONS IN THE SEA

Parina sought Borick amongst the ocean of faces, searched for him in the crowd that had thronged her, and found him in a corner, smiling encouragingly at her. Shooting a grateful smile in his direction, she started:

When the burning sun goes blind
Stopping his concerned rays from
Peeping at our joys and miseries;
When the reflecting moon loses her lustre,
Robbing the poets of their muse
And the lovers their moonlit romance;
When the powerful wind loses his strength,
Energy sapped abandons the sea
Unable to breathe the sea decays;
Only one thing can save the world.

Faith.
Faith is belief in success,
Not just stupid, mindless belief
But knowledge, a confident wisdom.
Faith may not open the sun's eyes.
But warmth will find its way back.
Faith may not make the moon glow
But love and romance will return.
Faith may not churn the sea
But the decaying will stop.
Faith is not depending on another
But believing in yourself.
Believe that you already possess it and you will.
Faith lives not on an uncertain 'I can do it'
But in a confident 'I will do it'
Have faith and your wish is willed into success.

The school listened, as keen as ever. Whoever could nod nodded at regular intervals. Whoever could not, thumped their tails. 'Aye, Aye,' they said. Faith can do many things but who has the time for faith, was their singular thought. Chasing and eating prey, alert with omnipresent eyes to save the skin is all we have time for. Who has time to think of faith, they thought—with great unity of thought.

But they listened nevertheless. They didn't understand half of what she spouted. The part about the poets and the muses and lovers romancing in moonlight swam over their heads. Not topics the creatures of the sea were well versed in.

But, of course, they listened. Some casually interested, some out of curiosity. Reverent eyes fixed on the dolphin, spellbound. She was the only creature who'd lived in a different world and returned to re-live it with them.

All creatures, big and small, innocent and cunning, preys and predators—gathered in effortless gobbling distance of each other—unconcerned about being eaten up, unmindful of their daily manoeuvres that kept them alive, were thinking the same thought. Who has time for faith in our mundane life? What unity of mind in such diverse beings!

A little fish, Sera, lost in the world of the dolphin's recital, had taken time off to return to the watery world she was born in, and turned curiously to check on her poking rocky seat.

Hastily, without losing a second to ponder, with no visible trace of anxiety whatsoever, her composure perfectly intact, slowly and dextrously, Sera wove her way through the mesmerised gathering and managed to accommodate an appreciable distance between her and her hard chair.

The haste was masked not so as to offend her makeshift chair but because she did not particularly wish to announce her identity as a morsel of the daily diet of her until-now-underside-holder.

Throughout the dolphin's recital, Sera had been resting her rear portion right at the gate of a killer whale's mouth. And all the while, she had been waving her delectable orange tail in front of the whale's nose, almost baiting him into sampling her.

Gulping her heart back into its proper place, Sera sent a prayer to her Great God, who as an afterthought had saved her life, giving her the presence of mind just in time, before the inevitable fatal mishap occurred.

She thanked Him for today until now and prayed that He would let her last the day out, and if possible try and be generous and allow her one more day in this world she loved, before she was sucked into the dark cavern of a bigger creature's mouth.

Before again surrendering to the dolphin's hypnotic spell, Sera checked on her neighbours carefully and, comforted by their size and identity, gave her undivided attention to the dolphin's recital again.

Meanwhile the killer whale, unaware of the little fish's near-heart-seizure, was still listening attentively to the dolphin. And so was the rest of the gathering.

'Have faith and your wish is willed into success,' Parina repeated as she concluded. Cutting through the crowd, she reached Borick. 'How was I? Good?' she asked, her eyes dancing.

'Fabulous! But you hardly know how right you are. And, ma'am, you'll have to stop spouting poetry. Half your audience was sleeping, the other half looked dazed.'

'I know, I know,' she laughed, 'I tried but I couldn't help it. It all came out in verse. Maybe, I was a poet in my last life,' she sang happily.

'Like I said, you don't know how right you are,' he sighed.

Plodding back home, Borick suddenly turned to Parina and said, 'Parina, for the love of life, when are you going to stop this?'

'Stop what, Borick?' she asked, startled, a trifle scared by his vehemence.

'Your preaching, what else? You aren't a prophetess manifested in the sea, you know?' Borick taunted.

'Borick, I preach because I enjoy it. Not because I think of myself as a prophetess. I preach because I love the crowd. I love the thousand pairs of eyes gazing at me with that worshipful look. I love the thousand pairs of ears struggling to catch every word that I utter. I love the thousand minds that think that I'm wonderful. That is the reason why I preach. I preach because they love me, because they want me to preach.'

'I thought so,' he laughed humourlessly. 'You don't love the crowd, you love yourself. And that's where you're making a mistake. A preacher preaches because he loves the crowd as much as himself. He yearns to share his knowledge, to ease the pain. But you are not a prophet. You don't even know the answers you've come here for!' He barked again, a cruel laugh.

'Either way, the path that you're taking, you'll probably spend a million lives before you figure out that you're actually searching for something. You are so wrapped up in your own world!' he jeered.

'What rubbish!' Parina burst out and glided off, steaming in anger.

But he was close on her tail, adding gently, 'Parina, by craving for attention, you're depending on another. And that's not all right. The attention you seek from that crowd, you can find in yourself. When you know deep inside that you're a beautiful creature, believe me, it feels a lot better than a thousand voices shouting it out to you!'

Parina tried to ignore him, but his words managed to sink into her sensitive skin. Pretending she'd never heard a word he said, she went on without stopping. Borick knew he had touched a raw nerve. He hoped she would spend a sleepless night worrying about what he'd just said.

While she was gliding away, a thought bounced in her mind: *You're here on a mission, in search of something. Only when you find it, will you know*!

She wondered what she was in search of and after racking her brains for a couple of hours, gave up. Whatever it is, she would find it one day. Why worry now?

A DREAMTIME SEQUENCE

The next day, the sun rose with four equally sunny consorts. Five suns rode in the sky, the centre sun flanked by pairs of suns. Which is real? Which is an illusion? Which is something, which is nothing? Who is mocking whom? Is reality an illusion? Are they all real? Are they all an illusion?

Parina had never seen a spectacle like this before. A sky with five suns! She turned to Borick for an explanation. Borick was smiling like he knew the answer. Like he'd seen this happen before. She was about to plod him with her question when, seemingly out of nowhere, Arij burst upon them, his once black shiny body now a lifeless grey.

'Pari!' he gasped breathlessly and stopped, unable to speak further.

Concerned, Parina held him close and waited.

'Pari! They have taken her. Man has snatched my Cutra... Pariii...' he wailed and dissolved into tears.

Unable to see her friend in such a pitiable state and completely at a loss for words, Parina glanced at Borick.

Borick shifted towards Arij and, rubbing himself against the velvety body, asked, 'What happened, Arij?'

'Cutra, my sweet Cutra has been grabbed. They've trapped her, she's gone forever.'

'Don't be stupid. How can anyone take her away from you?' asked Borick impatiently. 'Have you lost her? Have you let her go?'

'Man has killed her, he's probably...' he gulped '... probably skinned her by now!'

'Have you killed her?' Borick deliberately goaded him.

'What do you mean? How can I kill her? I love her! How can I kill her? How can you say that!' His temper flared for an instant but fizzled in a maelstrom of sorrow. He began choking on his sobs.

'Stop that!'

Numb with pain, Arij quietened down.

'Arij, Cutra is not dead. If you don't want her to die, she won't. She is alive, in you, in me, everywhere... She is not dead, she is alive.'

Hypnotised by Borick's hope-filling words, Arij looked at Borick, eyes glazed, ready to believe anything, anything that would bring his love back.

'Close your eyes.'

'Umm.'

'Now what do you see?'

His mind was filled with Cutra, he could see nothing but her. He screwed his face tight, concentrating on the picture behind his eyes. His mouth curved into a mysterious smile. His Cutra was laughing, eyes twinkling. She was teasing him, biting his tail.

'Hey, Cutra! Stop that... it hurts,' he shouted in laughter. And then he turned and chased her all around the place, dodging the fish that darted blindly, bumping into a couple of them in his rush.

'Caught you!' he yelled, face flushed, trapping her on the seabed.

But Cutra wriggled free and escaped.

'See! She is alive, she is not dead.' Borick's voice seemed to come from a distance, and he forced his eyelids open.

Borick was indeed at a distance. Arij moved closer to him. His eyes soft as flowers, face fresh and radiant, he looked like the calm after a storm. He was exhausted, spent, but peaceful at last.

'See... only you can kill her. She is alive as long as you want her to live. Nobody can snatch her away from you. Only you have the power to let her go.'

Silence laid siege. Even the ocean sensing the mood breathed a regular splashing beat. They lapsed into a reflecting mood. Borick was calm and serene, his task accomplished. Parina was uneasy, her mind spinning with questions. Arij was well... Arij was meditating on what he'd just seen, he was lost in a different dimension. Without a word, he moved away further into the ocean.

Parina wanted to follow him, but Borick stopped her with a 'Let him be. Let him digest what he's just seen. I shouldn't have done it, I think, but he needed it.'

'But what did he see?' Parina asked puzzled. 'I didn't see Cutra.'

'Sweetheart, there's a difference between the way you see Cutra and the way he sees her. You see her as another seal but he sees beyond that. He sees wishing desperately to see her. He sees her with love's piercing eyes and love is a pretty powerful emotion. True love sees beyond the illusions we have inflicted on our lives. He sees his love, a piece of his soul, not a seal; therein lies the difference,' he explained and went off in search of an iceberg to meditate on.

You cannot die because you were never born. No one can hurt you or burn you or drown you and never will you grow old. You are beyond any law, beyond any obligation to anyone other than yourself, is what her inner mind told her.

Parina shrugged it off, a trifle uneasy. How does he know so much?

Her restless mind tossed the questions around and played with them. She scratched her mind and dug deeper. She saw the answer. She saw the restless walrus trudging up the mountain, in desperation shouting his questions, worrying his mind and then seeing the light.

She broke out in cold sweat as she recognised the look on his face. He looked like a sage. He had the face of a Buddha, a peaceful Shiva, a radiant Jesus. He had changed overnight. The realisation terrified her.

She spent a while, thinking, contemplating on her next move. She searched the skies for enlightenment.

The four suns had disappeared, leaving the real sun behind. She stared at the sun for a while, praying for an explanation. She listened to the ocean breathe, trying to find her silence in the ocean's repeated roar.

But her mind refused to be reined in. Unable to wait any longer for explanations, she looked for Borick and found him at the sea-mount. She pasted a smile on her face and approached him. Borick gave her a penetrating look, saw through the fake smile to the agitation in her mind.

Abandoning her pretence, she rushed up to him and asked, 'Borick, is it true?'

'The dream? The vision you had?' he asked and without waiting for her reply added, 'Yes, that is how it happened.'

'But why? Why you? There are millions of men and women who struggle and perform penance for enlightenment and all you have to do is walk up a mountain and lo and behold you're enlightened. It's so ridiculous.'

'What's so ridiculous? What do you think is behind all that penance? Concentration. Single-mindedly searching the mind, without getting distracted. You don't really have to stand on one leg, starve and let anthills grow all over you to answer a simple arithmetic problem. All you have to do is find the answer, work it out by yourself.

'There are different ways of arriving at the answer. You might at times end up with an entirely wrong one but work on it, persevere and you'll see the truth. It's a trial-and-error method, you see. Explore different ways and sure enough your curiosity will be satisfied. All paths lead to the same destination.

'The answer is right within you. But you're going to have to come up with it. It might take a while, a few lifetimes perhaps, or you might just crack it with one good try.

'I was restless for an answer so I walked up that mountain. I did not know if I would come back here alive. But I kept my mind focused on the matter, tried to survive, not wanting to destroy myself. Knowing I am special, that my life is a gift, that I have to fight to keep it alive, to go on because I am here to find the big answer. I was desperate enough, maybe open-minded enough. Something clicked, the fog lifted, lightning flashed...

'Look at that mountain,' he said abruptly.

Caught unawares by his sudden command, she did a swift pirouette to look at the mountain. It looked the same to her.

'Those birds!' he added, reading the question in her mind.

She looked at the birds. Some were sitting right on top. Some were a level below. Some others were way below the rest. Some were enjoying flight, silhouetted against the sky. She turned back again with a 'what's new' look in her eyes.

'Each bird is on a different level and it's entirely up to them whether they want to go higher or stay where they are—comfortable in their surroundings. A more inquisitive bird flies higher than the rest and sees better sights.

'For every mountain, there is a higher mountain, the highest one touching the stars. The one that reaches the stars looks down upon the whole world and revels in its knowledge.

'That's the way it is—entirely your choice. Reach for the stars, grow. Or stay where you are happy and contented. The ones you call foolish or dumb are presently on a lower level. If they choose to, they can fly higher. They have wings, they have the power. What they need is the will to soar, an imagination to dream of higher heights. That's the way it is. Mind power. Soul power. A higher spirit.'

Parina peered at him intently. She was aware of all the things he'd just said. But hadn't actually believed it worked. Believing in his philosophy would probably decimate her identity as a dolphin. Not that she enjoyed being a dolphin. She would rather be a Man any day! But even Man didn't believe in this philosophy. He'd written the idea down in his primitive days but times have changed now, and he has grown smarter. Can't really have the birds, fish, monkeys, donkeys and amoebas believing they are at par with humans and acting accordingly, can you? Imagine fish walking, pigs flying! The world will not be the same any more. It will turn into a wonderland, a fairyland, where anything can happen anytime. Anyone can be anything they want to be... Oh well, they don't even want to treat themselves as equals. Each thinks they're superior and they are so quick to pull another one down.

Nevertheless, equality amongst all beings is not a bad idea at all, she thought. It would give the dolphins a chance to know the stability of solid ground where gravity does its bit for the planet. They could rejoice that no wave could push them around to places they never intended to go to.

Grinning at the picture she'd conjured up, she shook her head at the sheer absurdity of it all. Borick was watching her, she knew, so she looked at him and grinned. He grinned back. 'Why not? Fish can walk and pigs can fly!' he said, eyes dancing mischievously. 'One day, sweetheart, I'll show you how!' he promised and plodded away.

Parina stared at his retreating back pensively. She pondered on his words and convinced herself that it was too crazy to believe in. 'Pigs flying!' She made a face and turned towards her sea-mount. On the way, she caught a squid and gobbled her up after mumbling a thanks.

THE END BEGINS

'Know something? An hour back, I would never have believed it but now I kind of think it's possible to change form. Do you really believe it's possible, this changing form business? Can pigs fly? Can fish walk on land?' she asked after trying to convince herself that it was possible. She wasn't thoroughly convinced but was putting on a nice show of having been convinced. She wanted to know if it was possible, if Borick could do it.

'Of course, it's possible. If you believe it's possible then anything is. We don't believe strongly enough and that's why nothing gets done. Changing form is easy. Perhaps, one day...' Borick stopped suddenly. 'But what do you want to become? A Man? A human being?'

'Yes! I want to be a human. Want to know why? To walk. I want to hold my head high. I want to walk into my old room and switch on the television. I want to go

to the library my Master used to go to and read books. The hitch is I can't read. But I guess, if I can learn to change form, learning to read won't be such a difficult task... I'll learn or ask someone to read it out for me.

'Oh! If only it can be done,' she wailed, hoping he would take the hint.

Borick, of course, knew her game, but played along. 'If someone told you that he could turn you into a Man now, would you still want to be one or would you back out, terrified of the unknown dangers?'

'Of course, I would dive at the idea! Think I'm joking? Moreover, I never get scared!'

'All right then... I know the secret behind changing forms and pulling rabbits out of hats. I can do it for you. Only I want you to believe it's possible,' he said and before she could think of wondering at him for knowing such secrets, he added, 'Close your eyes and imagine you are a human being in that library you want to be in. Picture it and you are there,' he said.

Parina did as told. A feeling of weightlessness spread through her. She flew through space, out of her body, unrestricted yet guided by some unknown force. She suddenly realised what it felt like to be a blind man and a bird at the same time. Guided yet free. She wanted to see where she was going, so she opened her eyes and all she saw were books, books and books, neatly stacked on racks.

She turned to her left. Borick was nodding at a gentleman in a brown coat. The gentleman showed no sign of bewilderment. He acted like he knew Borick. Maybe he's blind, she thought, trying to reason it out. And unable to differentiate between a walrus and a man.

Her underside was hurting. Shuffling ever so slowly, she ambled across to the books.

'Borick, where are we?'

'Where did you want to go?'

'To a library? Am I dreaming?'

'Wait! I'll do the pinching for you!' Without waiting for an answer, he poked her cheek.

Opening her mouth to scream, she realised that they would be drawing unwanted attention. She clamped her mouth shut.

A thought assaulted her and she looked down. No, she hadn't grown any legs, she could only see the floor. Through the corner of her eye, she could see her dolphin body suspended in thin air, while her eyes were on level with the fourth rack.

'Borick, where are we?' she asked urgently this time.

'In the library, where else?' he asked, a roguish smile playing on his lips.

'How did we get here? Have you cast a spell on me? Hypnotised me?'

'You do it all to yourself. Every living moment you spend, you're hypnotising yourself. Believing just what you want to believe.'

'Listen…!' she started in exasperation. She wasn't sure she was ready for a lecture in a library.

'Yes! But now, I have hypnotised you. Made you believe exactly what I want you to believe. And you're seeing just what I want you to see—an ordinary library filled with books and some people.'

'Miracles? Magic?' she asked, ignoring the last part that sounded like a brag.

'No miracles, no magic! A magician's work is no longer magic for him. It's a practical application of the theories you find in your physics book. You've lived with a scientist for so many years, you should have figured it all out by now.'

'He never had the time for me...' she mumbled under her breath.

'Whatever! His books were read out, weren't they?'

'Okay, so I'm dumb?' she flared up.

'Tut, tut, my baby, don't burst a vessel. You know you aren't dumb so don't fish for compliments. The problem with you is you don't apply your mind. I've been trying to explain so many things, but you choose to ignore them. It's like you want to learn at your own pace. Can't fault you on that though.'

Parina was irked. She sensed the contempt in his tone, but it wasn't the time or the place for a scene. She swallowed the rising bile with enormous difficulty. Sarcasm, however, crept into her voice and with fake reverence she asked, 'O Enlightened One, Your devoted servant seeks Your wisdom. Pray, please do explain this miracle. How have You deluded me into believing I'm in a library?'

Ignoring the sarcasm, Borick said, 'Let's assume that you're standing on your tail and a frisbee is balanced on your beak. What happens if you slowly move your beak?'

'The frisbee falls.'

'Oh!? Okay. Now, supposing, your Master puts his finger under a frisbee and moves his finger without upsetting the frisbee. Tell me what happens to the frisbee?'

'The frisbee moves with the finger.'

'The frisbee changes position, all because a point under the frisbee has been moved. Similarly, I have moved a part of you, the essential part of you, into this illusion of a library and so even your body has followed,' Borick explained.

'So? A walrus and a dolphin coolly amble into a library and not one of the fifty people present stop to give a second look? Okay, wait! I'll try that again! Correct me if I'm wrong. They believe they are seeing human beings, so they are! But hang on! Something doesn't fit. I know that I'm a dolphin so I still see my dolphin body but how is it that I can reach the fourth rack? That's impossible with a dolphin body, isn't it?' she asked half to herself.

'There you'll have to blame me,' he replied nonchalantly.

'Have you deluded my body into behaving like a human being?' she asked, trying to believe it.

'Yes, milady! Your own learned master pleads guilty.' He tried putting on a forlorn, repentant expression but couldn't pull it off too well. 'I just couldn't resist it. You were so eager to come to this library,' he grinned like a naughty devil.

Her mind started spinning again. 'Take me back,' she urged suddenly.

'Sure.'

And then they flew through time and space again. Before she knew it, she was in the ocean. And Borick was playing with the waves.

'Gosh! That was crazy!' and then she remembered how it all began.

'Where is Arij?' she asked. 'Haven't seen him since that Cutra episode.'

'He's trying to meet Cutra again.'

'But Cutra is dead.'

'Not exactly. Cutra is now a human being.'

'Oh! And Arij?'

'Arij is also a human being. He stopped being a seal yesterday.'

'You mean he's dead too.'

'No, he's born again. Evolved.'

'I want to be a human being,' she said urgently.

'You were a human being.'

'No, not for two minutes, faked by you! I want to be born as a human being.'

'You were a human being in your last birth. You've graduated.'

'No, I want to be a human being in this life too. I want to meet my Master.'

'Your Master is doing time again. He made a mistake the last time he was there. He kept you against your will.'

'But I wanted to be there!'

'No! You wanted to be here,' he corrected her, he knew.

'Anyway, I want to be a human being.' Parina was adamant.

'Then you'll have to wait to be reborn as a human being,' he shrugged.

'You're sure I'll be born again as a human being?'

'Well, yes, if that's what you want. But I think it's a foolish move. You know you are better than them. You are beautiful. You spread joy, you make everyone wonder why they can't be happy, you make them smile involuntarily, you spread laughter, you're here to teach everyone to love one another. Humans have to kill trees or use complicated gadgets if they want to communicate with someone out of their reach. You are a step ahead; you know how to transplant thoughts. You are evolved, you learnt their language. Nobody out there came up to your level and learnt yours. Why do you want to throw it all away? You're almost there, almost home.'

'I can transplant thoughts?' She'd stopped there.

'Haven't you realised it yet? I have always heard what you were thinking. Ever since you moved into my world... Whenever you were agitated, your thoughts spilled over to mine.'

'Oh? But why you?'

'Maybe because I knew I had something to learn from you and I wanted to listen. It's all a chain, you see, we seek out whoever we need to learn from. Through experiences we grow.'

She clicked in exasperation. 'We're rambling again. I want to be a human being.' A thought interrupted her other thoughts. Would Borick be hurt and lonely if I died? Maybe that's why he's telling me not to?

'No. I'll miss your physical presence, but you'll always be there for me. And so will I, for you. You have my unconditional love,' he replied, as though she'd voiced her fears aloud.

After a while, Parina turned and with a last look, swam away.

Borick knew he had to carry on with his life's purpose. Breathing deeply, purposefully with a pattern, he began his work. A golden light spread in the ocean as he started to transmit thoughts and energy, empowering the waterworld. The moment the golden light touched the ocean life, they felt confident. From the next moment, everything around them appeared breathtakingly beautiful.

Fish swimming around would suddenly stop and stare at the colours in the ocean, at the beauty in the ugliness of a jellyfish's tentacles. Jellyfish would forget to startle poor unsuspecting fish and marvel at their scales instead. Instead of being scared of sharks and quickly darting away, the fish would go closer and inspect the shark's teeth—the shape, the size and the sharpness. The shark would look on kindly, having forgotten to eat. In all, aquatic life lost the memory of preying. Fear no longer had a place in the ocean. Everyone had discovered the joy of living, of loving.

Borick worked tirelessly—sending the golden light out night and day. Soon, he started seeing fish playing chase, oysters laughing as they dropped tears on their pearls. The fish created plays about situations that had earlier frightened them to death. In these, sharks and walruses would pretend to be scared of the puny fish and run amok while the fish snapped at their fins. What used to be unthinkable turned into a game. It was almost like hunger didn't exist any more. They could live on love and fresh air. And they could have lived indefinitely if they wanted to. But sometimes, an occasional fish or a clam or a crab would stop seeing the beauty all around, get bored or just lose the enthusiasm. That's when it would drop dead. The birds would then quickly carry the dead away.

So it was with Parina. Convinced that she could be truly alive only as a human being, the dolphin lost the desire to live. She peacefully died in her sleep while dreaming of life as a human.

Borick saw it all. Parina had been released into the ocean for a purpose. Fate had ordained it, but she'd exerted her free will wishing to return to land. Her memories, her habits, her desires had overruled her fate. He knew, he understood. In his world, there was no forgiveness since there was no hurt or pain. He also knew that without knowing it, she'd trained him to fulfil his purpose and hers. She'd inspired him. He'd learnt from her and, yes, she was his soulmate. They didn't need to be together; they were part of each other.

After forty days of non-stop work, Borick was pleased with the changes he'd wrought in his world. He was done, ready to leave. He shifted himself to the mountain peak he had scaled earlier and sat there, eyes closed, breathing love—inside out.

THE NEW BEGINNING

Borick never came down from the mountain. Summer turned into winter. Light stubbed itself out, darkness ruled. Days pulled themselves into weeks, weeks grew to long months, months spread their roots into months, years sprouted years and slipped into decade. Decades crept into scores. Time took its toll. The wind ate his flesh, the snow froze his bones, his bones turned into a rock. He sat there on the peak, staring at the stars.

Fiona O'Conner came crying into her new world. She grew up somewhere on an Irish coast, the daughter of a fisherman. She was an only child, so she spent most of her early days with her father sailing on the sea, laughing at the dolphins bobbing on the waves, swimming with them, feeling like a mermaid.

She has graduated into a cetacean expert; she spends her time researching whales and dolphins. She believes dolphins are the most evolved creatures on earth. She knows that dolphins talk through telepathy, see with sonar beams. She envies them, she wants to be like them. They look so cheerful, so happy, as if life is a beautiful gift. This is the way I want to live, she dreams. She doesn't know she has an ancient bond with them, but yet, she knows. Her soul knows and feels the joy when she connects with them.

Of course, there are times when life tries to yank her down into its dregs of despair. Then Fiona pulls herself together and heads out to her favourite haunt. She goes to a particular snow-covered mountain on a little isle, up north in the ocean. She smiles fondly at the seals and walruses sunning themselves. *I am the egg man,* she grins as she remembers her favourite childhood song. *I am the walrus.* She leaves them behind as she strides her way to the top. She sits on a certain boulder and looks down upon the harsh, cruel world.

At times, she lies on her back listening to the ballad of the northern lights. Most often, she lies upside down, pressing her fresh tender bosom to the hard rock. Heart on heart, cheek to cheek, she pours her fears out, confiding her anxieties, seeking advice. She listens to the rock. It soothes her mind, calms her restlessness, stills her butterfly heart, makes her peaceful once again, and makes her feel one with the universe. When her eyes open, she fears nothing and she stops blinking. A strange smile spreads across her face and lights up her eyes. She begins to laugh again, at her outrageously funny life, at what is and what is not.

**All stories do not end as the book ends.
Parina would like to continue
the conversation with you.**

Hello, I am Parina, the strange dolphin in the story you just finished reading! So far, I have conducted schools of fish, and this is the first time I am talking to school-going children. Did you know that we are considered to be one of the most intelligent creatures with impressive social skills second only to you humans?

We may appear to be squeaking, whistling, clicking or making crazy noises when we speak to each other. But that is how you sound to us when you speak too. Anyway, let me find out how much you know about us.

Take the Dolphin Quiz below:

1. Are dolphins fish or mammals?
2. If a group of owls is called a parliament, then what is a group of dolphins called?
3. Which is the largest dolphin in the world?
4. Can you name the smallest dolphin in the world?
5. What do dolphins eat?
6. Should we feed wild dolphins?
7. Name the most famous dolphin in the world?

**Answers are on the next page*

Answers:

1. Dolphins are social mammals who interact with one another, swim together, protect each other, and hunt for food as a team.
2. A pod.
3. The Orca, also known as the killer whale, is the largest member of the dolphin family. Its black-and-white patterned body is very distinctive.
4. Hector's dolphins are the smallest dolphin species in the world. They are found only in New Zealand. They have distinct black facial markings, short stocky bodies and a dorsal fin shaped like a Mickey Mouse ear.

5. Fish, squid, jellyfish and crustaceans such as crab, lobster, shrimp and barnacle.
6. No. Feeding them makes them dependent on us, and this can lure them to dangerous areas of the shore.
7. Flipper, a bottlenose dolphin, the star of a widely loved and extremely popular TV series titled *Flipper,* as well as three films. In the TV series, Flipper is an extraordinarily intelligent pet dolphin with a remarkable understanding of human nature who almost invariably foils illegal activities in the marine reserve (Florida, USA) where he lives.